COMFY SQUAD

COMFY PRINCESS CAPERS

By **Suzanne Francis**

Illustrated by **Denise Shimabukuro** and the **Disney Storybook Art Team**

Random House 🏠 New York

rhcbooks.com
ISBN 978-0-7364-4187-2 (trade)
MANUFACTURED IN CHINA
10 9 8 7 6 5 4 3 2 1

The Internet versions of the Disney Princesses lived inside the website OhMyDisney.com. They had just wrapped up another round of the quiz "Which Princess Would Be Your BFF?" and were taking a break.

Suddenly, a strange light flickered inside the princesses' dressing room as **Vanellope von Schweetz** appeared.

"Uh, hi," she said, looking at the stunned women.

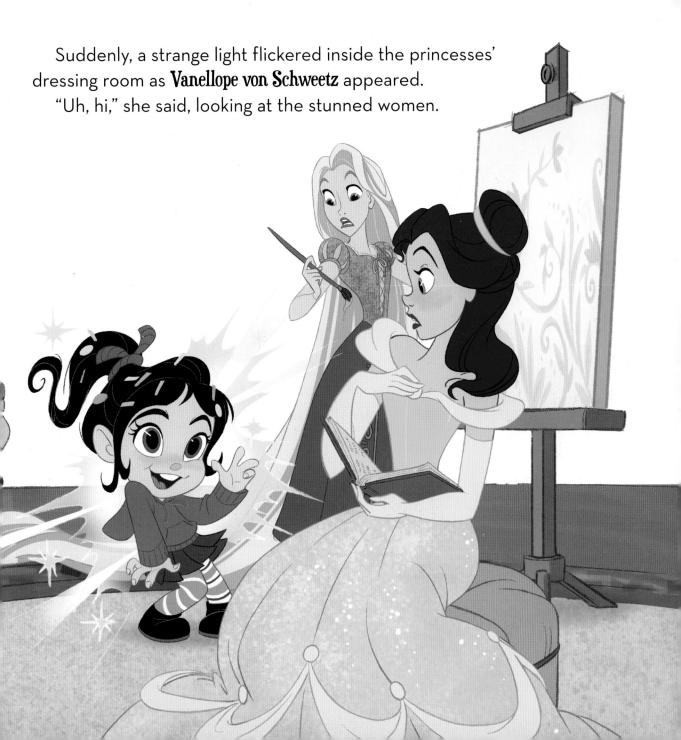

They sprang into action, ready to attack the stranger!
"Whoa-whoa, ladies . . . ," said Vanellope. "I can explain.
See, um, I'm a princess, too. Princess Vanellope von Schweetz,
of the *Sugar Rush* von Schweetzes."

Cinderella eyed Vanellope's outfit. "Who made your gown?" she asked. "I've never seen anything quite like it. I'd so love to have one of my own."

The other princesses agreed.
"Oh, I want one, too, you guys!" said **Ariel**.
"I'll get my mice on this," Cinderella said.

Soon each princess was lounging in a new outfit.
"So this is love," Cinderella said. "All hail Princess
Vanellope, the Queen of Comfy!"
"Yay, Vanellope!" they cheered.

Everyone enjoyed hanging out, but it wasn't long before a security guard knocked on the door—it was quiz time again.

"I guess it's back to the gowns, girls," said **Tiana** with a sigh.

Vanellope said goodbye to her new friends and set off.

The princesses gathered backstage. Everyone stared at Ariel, who was still in her comfy clothes!

"I couldn't do it," said Ariel. "I haven't had feet for very long, so I really like feeling them."

The princesses heard the announcer's voice welcoming a little girl to the site. "Greetings, young royal," he said. "Let's find out which princess you are!"

The girl took her time reading each question carefully. She made sure to pick the answers that represented her.

Finally, the announcer said, "Based on your answers, you're—Ariel!"

Ariel stepped into the spotlight, taking her place as the winner.

ARIEL

"A princess like you is a dream come true," she told the little girl's avatar.

Suddenly, the site went offline. A recorded voice said over and over,

"DRESS CODE ALERT!"

Wardrobe netizens, the characters that lived and worked in the Internet, appeared before Ariel.
"You gotta be in the gown."

"Fine," said Ariel. "But the clothes don't make the princess!"

After a long day, the princesses dove right back into their comfy clothes, ready for a night of relaxation and fun.

It was **Jasmine's** turn to cook dinner. Elsa and Pocahontas offered to help.

The others enjoyed some of their typical evening activities, like dance-offs and arm wrestling.

"Dinnertime!" Jasmine sang. "It looks like the picture, right?"

"Uhm . . ." Tiana turned her head to look at it differently. "Maybe?"

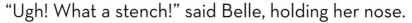

"Ugh! What a stench!" said Belle, holding her nose.

Mulan gagged. "That looks worse than army food!"

They hurried downstairs to their favorite restaurant instead.

After the princesses placed their order, **Eeyore** inched toward the tray, ready to take a big bite.

Suddenly, there was a distant rumbling.

"I think it's outside," Cinderella said.

The princesses exchanged looks before heading out the door.

On the patio, the noise grew louder.
The ground quaked as a stampede of
Wreck-It Ralph clones rushed by!

Snow White spotted a security guard.

"Excuse me," she said. "Can you tell us what's happening?"

"It's a virus," said the guard. "Apparently, it's moving pretty fast . . . attacking the entire Internet."

"Look!" said **Pocahontas**. "It's Vanellope!"

Vanellope gave her princess pals an update. The virus had created clones of her best friend, Wreck-It Ralph. "And they're trying to get me!" she said before racing off.

"We have to help," said **Rapunzel**, her mouth full.
Everyone agreed.
Snow White gasped. "Maybe if we find the real Ralph, we can stop it!"
"Good idea, Snow White," said **Belle**.

The princesses were ready to fight the virus. But buildings began crumbling around them.

"Watch out!" shouted Rapunzel. She used her frying pan to smack some falling rubble away from **Merida**.

Anna jumped into the air to avoid some falling train cars.

Elsa shot out an icy blast. A slide formed beneath Anna's feet. She coasted down and did an impressive twist and flip before gracefully landing on the ground.

Just then, Rapunzel saw the real Ralph falling from the top of a towering website!

"Why, it's a big strong man in need of rescuing!" she exclaimed.

The princesses instantly knew how to use their talents to slow Ralph's fall.

Tiana scanned the area, looking for one last thing. She and Anna hurried inside a shop and found some very familiar dresses.

"Mind if we borrow these?" they asked.

"I—I'd be honored," the salesperson stammered.

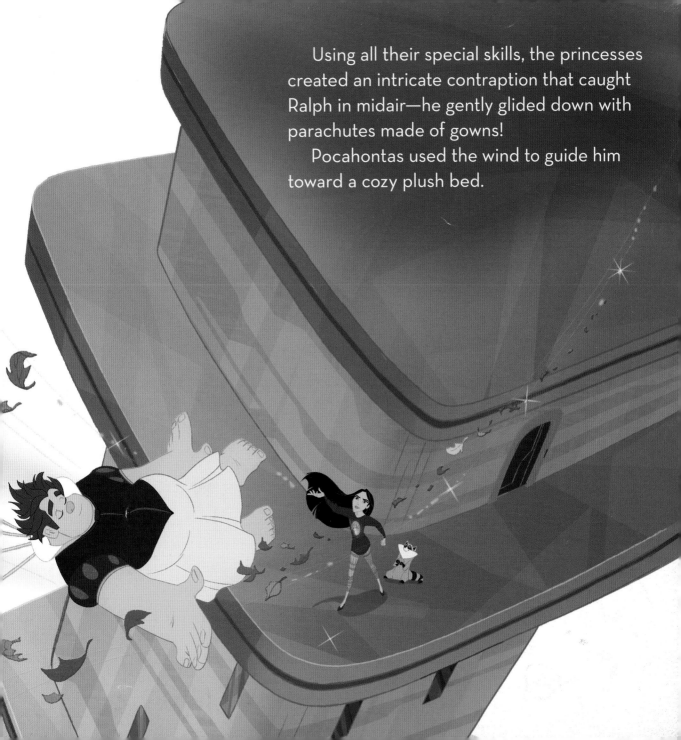

Using all their special skills, the princesses created an intricate contraption that caught Ralph in midair—he gently glided down with parachutes made of gowns!

Pocahontas used the wind to guide him toward a cozy plush bed.

When Ralph awoke, he looked around, confused.
"Wait a minute—who are all of you?" he asked.
"We're friends of Vanellope's," explained Jasmine.
"And any friend of Vanellope's is a friend of ours," said Elsa.
"You're welcome," said Moana.

Vanellope thanked the princesses for saving her best friend.
They were happy to help, and even happier to hear that
Vanellope was planning to stay in the Internet!
"Maybe you can visit me in *Slaughter Race*,"
said Vanellope.
"Absolutely!" said **Aurora**.

"Portrait time!" shouted Rapunzel as she set up her easel.

"Pretty princess faces—blehhhhh!" said Vanellope, sticking out her tongue. Then they all made funny expressions as Rapunzel painted their portrait, capturing the moment forever.

Vanellope von Schweetz lived inside the popular online game *Slaughter Race*. She and her friends loved racing, but when the game went offline, most of them were happy to take a break.

Before heading off, Vanellope's good friend **Shank** asked, "Quick race before I split?" She held up a trophy. "Think you can take the hubcap from the champ?"

"You're on," said Vanellope, hopping into her car.

The two revved their engines and took off!

Shank was in the lead. Vanellope glitched and flew off the edge of a ramp, catching air. She landed backward for the win!
"Bam!" cheered Vanellope, jumping out of her car.

"Nice," Shank said, handing Vanellope the trophy. "Have fun with your visitors."

While Vanellope's game was updating, she had invited her princess friends from OhMyDisney.com to visit.

Just then, the princesses stood backstage at OMD waiting for a quiz called "Favorite Princess Quotes" to wrap up.

Tiana stepped onto the stage. "If you do your best, each and every day, good things are sure to come your way," she told a child's avatar.

"If I do my best, the good thing coming my way is a nap!" said **Aurora** backstage. The others laughed.

"Is it time to go to *Slaughter Race*?" asked **Rapunzel**.

"I can't wait to see Vanellope!" **Mulan** said.

Meanwhile, Vanellope prepared for their arrival. She hunted for the perfect vehicles.

"I can see **Ariel** ripping up the road in you, my feisty little two-wheeler," she said, choosing a motorcycle for her friend.

She eyed a monster truck thoughtfully.
"You're saying to me . . . **Moana**."

Once they had finished for the day, the princesses rushed home.
When **Snow White** emerged, she was wearing something new.
"Where did you get that?" asked **Cinderella**.
"My mice sew, too!" said Snow White.

"Welcome, ladies!" said Vanellope when the princesses entered *Slaughter Race*.

"This is going to be so much fun, you guys!" **Merida** exclaimed.

Some princesses, like **Jasmine**, were eager to drive.
Others just wanted to go for a ride.
 "We do need new outfits," Cinderella said.
 "My mice can help!" said Snow White.
Her furry friends quickly got to work.

Soon all the princesses were ready to race!

"First things first," said Vanellope. "Seat belt! Click it or ticket!"

"Ach!" said Merida, yanking at her seat belt.

"Next," continued Vanellope, "insert the key and turn it to start your engines."

Ariel cheered as her motorcycle roared to life.

Pocahontas and Snow White gasped as their roof began to go up and down.

"Oh, no! The roof broke!" said Pocahontas.

"It's a convertible," said Vanellope. "It's supposed to do that."

Vanellope explained that first they would drive around the small beginners' course. Tiana took off! She weaved around each cone and came to a screeching halt right at Vanellope's feet.

"Nice," said Vanellope, impressed. "Who's next?"

The princesses each took a turn.
Aurora's car jerked as she struggled to shift.
Ariel tried to find her balance
on the motorcycle.

Later, they gathered in a garage to discuss their driving experience.
"Sometimes my friends and I have our own races," said Vanellope.
"Whoever wins gets the trophy."
"How wonderful!" exclaimed Cinderella.
"We should have a race," suggested Tiana.

"For a trophy!" added Jasmine.

"I like the way you're thinking," said Vanellope. She figured she could quickly set up a racecourse.

The princesses cheered and hurried off to practice!

Vanellope found a twisted license plate on the ground and picked it up.

"I'd better get my crew on this," she said to herself.

"Make a trophy," she told them. "Bring it to me in an hour."

The crew nodded before leaving with the plate.

Next, she got to work creating the racetrack, keeping the design simple. She also enlisted the help of a clown friend.

"Thanks, **Walter**," she said gratefully as he lined the track with flags.

Meanwhile, the princesses explored the game in their vehicles.
Moana tested the limits of the monster truck.

Snow White and Pocahontas enjoyed the feel of
the wind whipping through their hair.

Rapunzel and **Belle** drove
to an overlook to charge their
solar panels.

Soon everyone was ready for the race. Vanellope invited spectators to the stands and told the racers to take their places. Everyone cheered.

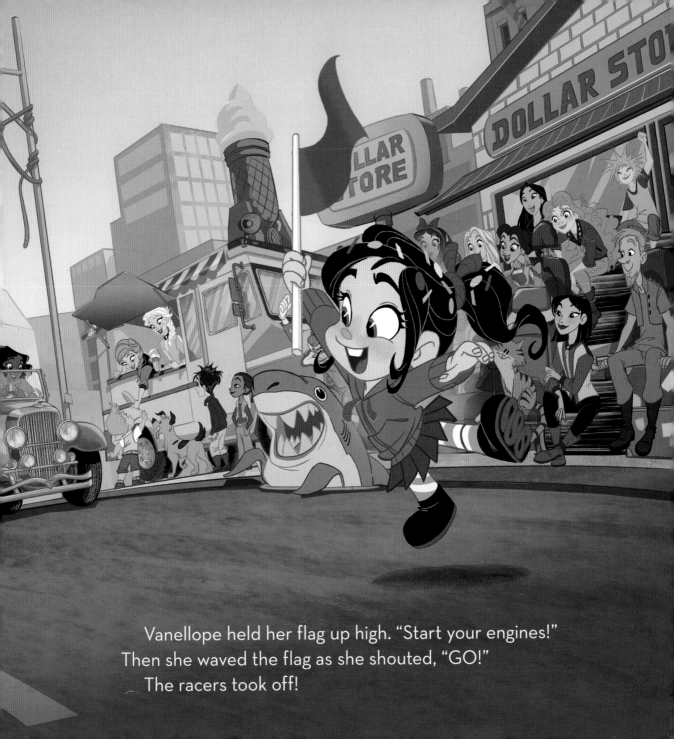

Vanellope held her flag up high. "Start your engines!"
Then she waved the flag as she shouted, "GO!"
The racers took off!

"Later, gators!" called Tiana, leaving them in the dust.
Cinderella quickly pulled up behind her.
Jasmine jammed on the gas pedal.
Aurora tried her best to catch up.

Cinderella hit a pothole, popping a tire!
She was out of the race.

Moana got stuck and was
out of the race, too.

Aurora cruised up beside Tiana. Tiana looked
over to see . . . that Aurora had fallen asleep!

"Wake up!" Tiana yelled.

But Aurora continued to snore.
Tiana tooted her horn. Driving while
sleeping was dangerous!

Aurora jolted awake just as she crossed
the finish line first! The crowd went wild!

Vanellope's crew carried
the trophy over.
Aurora was honored
to accept it.

Moments later, Shank returned from her break.
"Do you ladies want to go for a spin?" she asked.
"Hop in, everyone!" Vanellope said.
The princesses cheered as they excitedly
piled into the cars.

Afterward, Aurora turned to Shank. "You know," she said,
"we're only a few games away if you ever need an extra racer."
The princesses thanked Vanellope and Shank, then left,
dreaming about their next visit to *Slaughter Race*.